A Duck in New York City

Story and Songs by Connie Kaldor Illustrated by Fil & Julie

Once upon a pond there was a duck.
He was a little duck, but he had a big idea.
"I want to fly to New York City
and do my ducky dance on Broadway,"
said the little prairie duck.

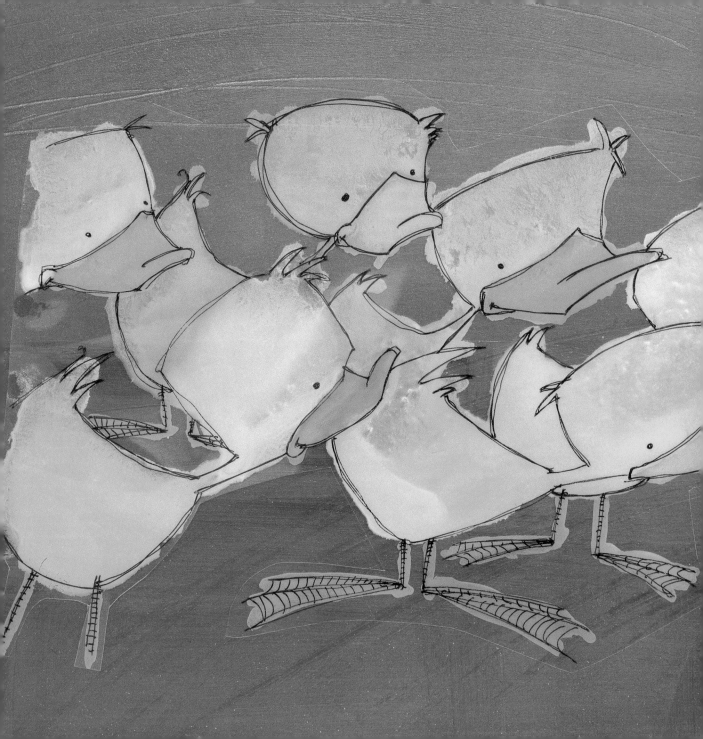

"New York City!" exclaimed the other ducks.
"You're too small. It's too far.
You can't go there."

But his brave little heart whispered,
"Yes, you can."

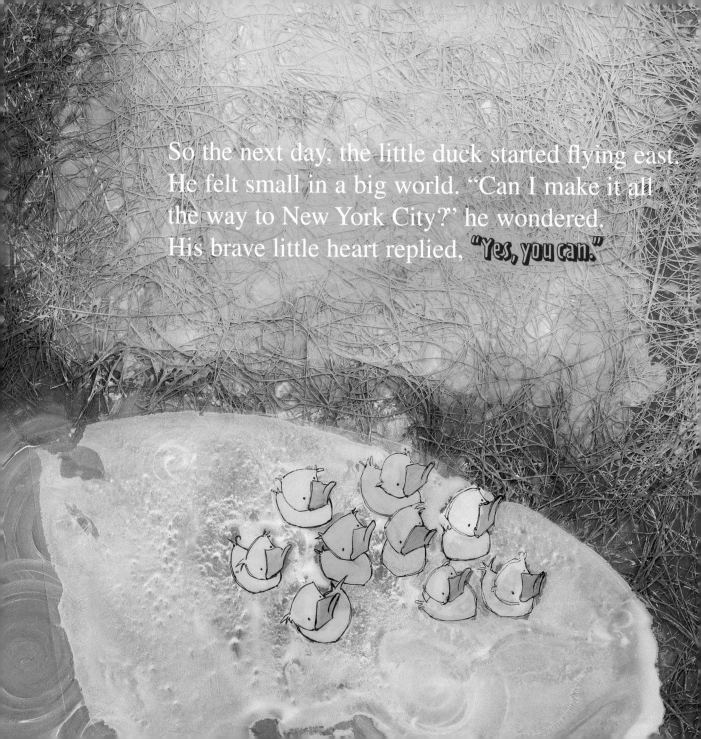

So the next day, the little duck started flying east.
He felt small in a big world. "Can I make it all
the way to New York City?" he wondered.
His brave little heart replied, **"Yes, you can."**

The little duck flew and flew
till he was all tuckered out.
Down, down, down he went,
looking for a soft place to land.

Bump!!! went the little duck
as he landed on a road.
"Oh no!" he cried. "What is this…
and what is that?"
Screech!!! went the big truck
as it came to a stop.

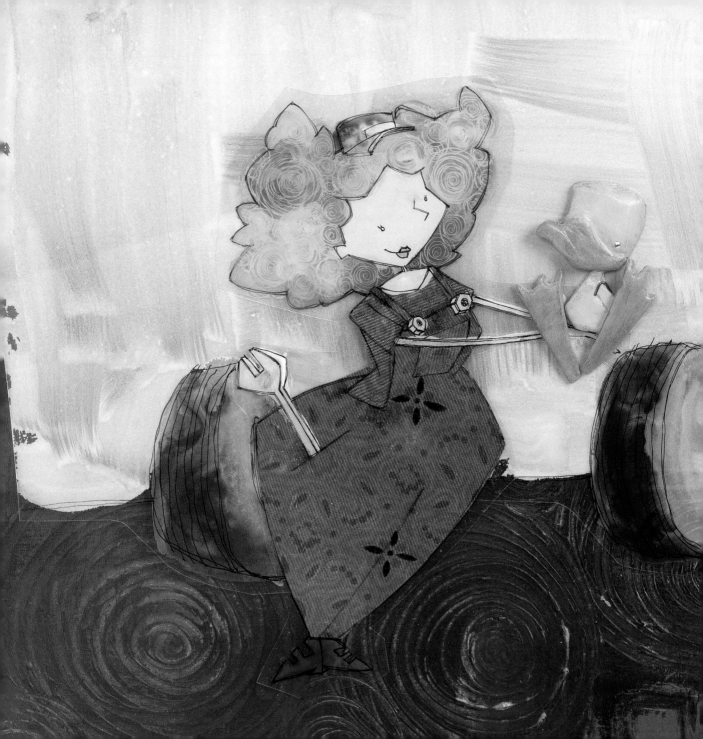

Out jumped the driver, Big Betty.
Big Betty loved big trucks,
big cups of coffee and little ducks.

"What's the big idea?" she asked. "The big idea," said the little duck, "is to dance my ducky dance on Broadway. Do you think I can do that?" Big Betty placed him gently on the dash of her truck and said, *"Yes, you can."*

At every truck stop along the way, the little duck performed his special dance.

One day, Big Betty stopped the truck,
turned to her little friend and said,
"I've got to head south. New York City
is that-a-way. Good luck little duck."

Through the wind and the rain he flew. **Yes, you can.** All the way to the tall buildings of New York. **Yes, you can.** Down, down, down to the heart of the big city. He had arrived! He couldn't believe his eyes…

There was the mayor waiting for him.
"Greetings little duck. I hear you've got
a big idea. Well, that's just ducky.
How about you doing that dance for us
on Broadway?"

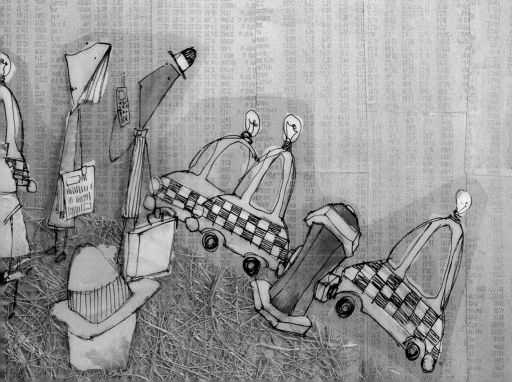

As the cameras flashed
and the people cheered,
the little duck sang out,
"Yes, I can!"

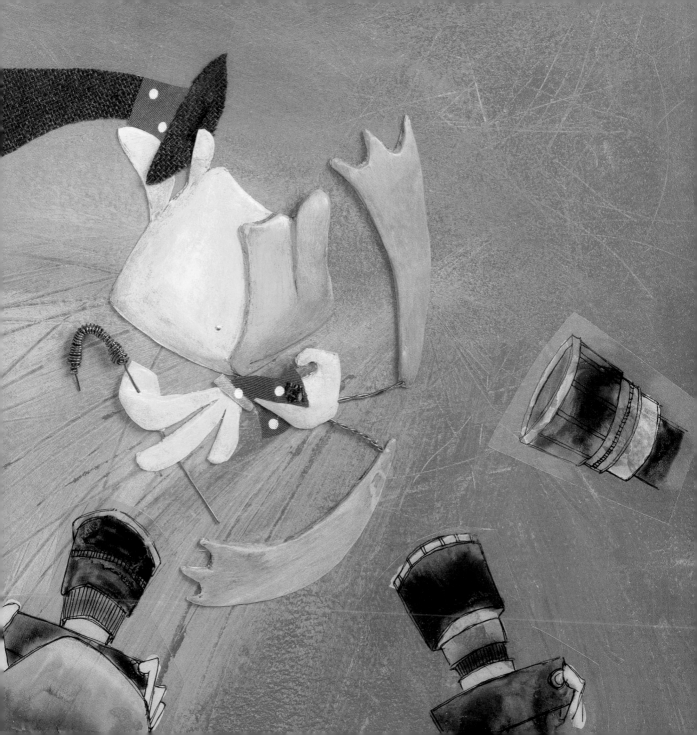

A Duck in New York City

There was a little duck in New York City ✳ Which is not exactly perfect for a duck ✳ Instead of little ponds with little lilies ✳ There are great big buildings, pavement and trucks ✳ But if you are a duck in New York City ✳ You do the very best with what you've got ✳ You don't go waddling after dark ✳ You take a taxi to the park ✳ And you find a fire hydrant when it's hot ✹ His apartment was too small to have a bathtub ✳ So he had to go out waddling on the street ✳ He'd pretend that he was swimming up the pavement ✳ Even though it often hurt his little feet ✳ But he loved to see the Nicks down at the Gardens ✳ And he loved the shows down on the Avenue ✳ And he says, "I feel at home in New York City ✳ 'Cause everyone is quackers too ✹ Start spreading the news ✳ I'm leaving today ✳ I want to be a part of it ✳ New York, New York ✹ So, if you are a duck in New York City… ✳ Oh yeah New York is ducky

"New York, New York" by Fred Ebb and John Kander (EMI Unart Catalog Inc.)

If You Love a Hippopotamus

If you love a hippopotamus ❋ And you love her a lot-amus ❋ She will be your friend (your friend) ❋ And that can be mighty handy now and then ❋ Cause if you're stuck outside ❋ And you find that the door won't budge ❋ Your friend the hippo can lean on it ❋ And give it that extra nudge ❋ Uuggghhhh ❋ Cause if you want a cookie ❋ But it's too high on the shelf ❋ You can climb on the back of a hippopotamus ❋ And get one for yourself… And one for her too ❋ Cause if you're put to bed ❋ And you find that you just can't sleep ❋ Your friend the hippopotamus into your room will creep ❋ And she'll sing you a lullaby 'til you begin to snore ❋ Then she'll tiptoe out hippopotamusly and slam the door ❋ Wham!

Laundry Bag

There were red socks and blue socks ❊ Odd socks, new socks in the laundry bag ❊ There are stretchy socks, white socks ❊ A bunch of left and right socks ❊ In the laundry bag ❀ And if you put your ear to the bag ❊ You can hear them say ❊ Give me some water, give me some soap ❊ And wash this dirt away ❀ There were red shirts, white shirts ❊ Even got a night shirt in the laundry bag ❊ There were plain shirts, checked shirts ❊ Ripped and kind of wrecked shirts in the laundry bag ❀ There were plain pants, party pants ❊ Even got some smarty pants in the laundry bag ❊ There were old jeans, new jeans ❊ Tina's favourite blue jeans in the laundry bag ❀ There were dishtowels, place mats ❊ Crazy Martian space hats in the laundry bag ❊ There were leotards and tutus ❊ Even a pair of running shoes in the laundry bag ❀ There's everything that I've worn for a month or so ❊ In the laundry bag

Belly Button

Belly button, belly button, my belly button ❊ My belly button I love you ❊ Belly button, belly button, my belly button ❊ My belly button, I love you ❀ Oh how sad and lonely I would be ❊ If when I lifted up my shirt I didn't see my ❀ You're the only friend I have - the one who really cares ❊ 'Cause every time I need you - you're always there ❀ When things get down, and looking kinda' grim ❊ I simply lift up my shirt and stick my finger in my ❀ There's one more thing that I would like to say ❊ I think that there should be a bellybutton day ❀ A day for belly buttons

The Alligator Waltz

The alligator waltz ❋ La-la-la-la hmmmmm ❋ The alligator waltz ❋ La-la-la-la hmmmmmm ❋ They come in groups of two ❋ Promising that they won't fight ❋ They hoochy kootchy kootchy koo ❋ Trying so hard not to bite ❋ It's tail-to-tail and nose-to-nose ❋ Oh-they love to hold each other close ❋ At the stroke of midnight ❋ They start swaying to and fro ❋ And by the swampy green moonlight ❋ You should see them dance the tango ❋ Sliding slowly and holding near ❋ Whispering romantic things in the ear ❋ The alligator waltz is quite the formal do ❋ It's tux and tails and fancy gowns ❋ And alligator shoes ❋ By the vine and cicada bug ❋ Boy can they ever cut the rug ❋ The alligator waltz is by invitation only ❋ And I'm afraid that you won't find ❋ An alligator who is lonely ❋ But if you hear on a swampy breeze ❋ A fast fox trot and a one, two, three ❋ The alligator waltz ❋ La-la-la-la hmmmmm ❋ It's the alligator waltz ❋ You can hear them humming in the moonlight ❋ To the alligator waltz ❋ I'll bet you didn't know an alligator could hum ❋ Did ya?

Seed in the Ground

If you've got the sun and if you've got the rain ❋ And you plant a little seed in the old back lane ❋ And you wish and you pray and you keep the weeds down ❋ You might find, ooh, you might find ❋ A root growing out from the seed in the ground ❋ A shoot growing out from the root from the seed in the ground ❋ A stem growing out from the shoot from the root from the seed in the ground ❋ A flower growing out from the stem from the shoot from the root from the seed in the ground ❋ A seed growing out from the flower from the stem from the shoot from the root from the seed in the ground

Slug Opera

Nobody likes us 'cause we're slugs ✹ No, they're not fond of us like they are of other bugs ✹ Nobody likes us 'cause we're slugs ✹ No, they're not fond of us like they are of other bugs ✹ But it's not our fault ✹ That we're slimy and brown ✹ It's not our fault ✹ That we're stuck on the ground ✹ It's not our fault ✹ But nobody wants to play ✹ With the kind of bug that Mother Nature made this way ✹ But it's not our fault ✹ There's slime wherever we go ✹ It's not our fault ✹ We're embarrassed too, y'know! ✹ It's not our fault ✹ But nobody seems to see ✹ That we're the kind of bug that's got personality ✹ Ah, but when the moon is clear ✹ And the night is right ✹ We grow little feet ✹ And we dance all night ✹ We got a little slug singer ✹ She's got a little slug song ✹ We got a little slug band ✹ We play all night long ✹ Well, our skins turn blue ✹ And we lose our slime ✹ And some of us even sparkle ✹ Some of the time ✹ But at the first sight of sun ✹ They disappear ✹ And we're back to being slimy and brown ✹ Way down here ✹ And nobody likes us 'cause we're slugs ✹ No, they're not fond of us like they are of other bugs ✹ Nobody likes us 'cause we're slugs ✹ No, they're not fond of us like they are of other bugs

Honey, Honey, Honey

There was a great big bear ✻ That climbed up a great big tree ✻ Looking for his favorite thing ✻ Honey ✻ Honey, honey, honey, honey, honey ✿ He climbed out on a limb ✻ As careful as can be ✻ And made a piece of toast to have some ✻ Honey ✻ Honey, honey, honey, honey, honey ✿ There was a hole in the tree and ✻ Out came a little bee ✻ He'd spent all summer long making his ✻ Honey ✻ Honey, honey, honey, honey, honey ✿ The bear said, "Mr. Bee ✻ I've toast as you can see ✻ And I would like to take all of your ✻ Honey ✻ Honey, honey, honey, honey" ✿ The bee said, "Mr. Bear, ✻ I've lots and I can share but ✺ I can't give you all of my ✻ Honey ✻ Honey, honey, honey, honey, honey." ✿ The bear said, "Mr. Bee ✻ I'm big as you can see ✻ And I'll reach in and take all of your ✻ Honey ✻ Honey, honey, honey, honey, honey." ✿ Now, when a bee stings a bear on the nose ✻ Down and down he goes ✻ He falls to the bottom of the tree without his ✻ Honey ✻ Honey, honey, honey, honey, honey ✿ And from that very day ✻ So the squirrels say ✻ The bear would always eat his toast with ✻ Jam ✻ Jam, jam, jam, jam, jam!

I Love Tomatoes

I love tomatoes ✻ I love tomatoes ✻ You can keep your carrots and potatoes ✻ I love tomatoes ❀ I've got tomatoes in my pocket ✻ Tomato coloured clothes ✻ I carry a tomato everywhere I go ✻ I've got tomatoes on my windowsill ✻ Tomatoes on my bed ✻ I sleep each night with a tomato on my head ❀ I love tomato cookies, I love tomato cake ✻ I love tomatoes in my salad ✻ And tomato milk shakes ✻ I like tomatoes in my cereal ✻ Tomatoes with my tea ✻ I like tomato flavoured toothpaste and tomato fricassee ❀ I even go so far as to sing off key ✻ And I sing so loud la la la la la ✻ And I don't listen to the music la la la la ✻ And then they start to boo ✻ And then they throw tomatoes at me ❀ T-O-M-A-T-O ☀ In my garden that's all I'll grow ✻ Cherry or Roma I love them so ✻ T-O-M-A-T-O

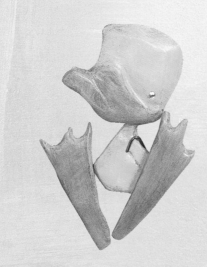

The Nose Song

I've got two feet ☀ Ain't that sweet ☀ But I've only got one little nose ☀ I've got two hands ☀ But I can't understand ☀ Why I've only got one little nose ❀ I sometimes wish I had two ☀ I like my nose so well ☀ I don't like it much when it sniffles ☀ But I love it when it smells ❀ I've got ten toes ☀ But wouldn't ya' know ☀ I've only got one little nose ☀ I've got two knees ☀ If you please ☀ But I've only got one little nose ❀ I've got two ears so I can hear ☀ But I've only got one little nose ☀ I've got two eyes and it's no surprise ☀ But I've only got one little nose ❀ I've got two feet ☀ Ain't that sweet ☀ But I've only got one little nose

Quack, Quack, Quack

Quack, quack, quack sings the little yellow ducky ❀ Quack, quack, quack is the yellow ducky song ❀ Quack, quack, quack sings the little yellow ducky ❀ Quack, quack, quack is the yellow ducky song ❀ All day long he loves to sing ❀ Loves to sing the same old thing, just ❀ Quack, quack, quack sings the little yellow ducky ❀ Quack, quack, quack is the yellow ducky song ❀ Boom, Boom, down in the barnyard ❀ Down in the barnyard, boom ❀ Baa, Baa, Baa sings the little white lamby ❀ Baa, Baa, Baa is the little lamby song ❀ Oink, oink, oink sings the little pink piggy ❀ Oink, oink, oink is the little piggy song ❀ Woof, woof, woof sings the little black doggy ❀ Woof, woof, woof is the little doggy song ❀ Meow, meow, meow sings the little fuzzy kitty ❀ Meow, meow, meow is the little kitty song

I Want to be a Cloud

When I grow up I want to be a cloud ❀ And float up in the sky above the crowd ❀ I'd be on the lookout for someone just like me ❀ Who's looking up into the sky to see what she can see ❀ I'd go ahead and puff myself up in the shape of things ❀ Like a tricycle or a hamburger or a giant diamond ring or ❀ A space ship, a whale or a penguin or a giant hat ❀ Then everyone would stop and say ❀ "Will you look at that?" ❀ Yes, when I grow up I want to be a cloud ❀ And float up in the sky above the crowd ❀ I'd rain upon the flowers just to watch them grow ❀ I'd only bring the gentle rain ❀ I'd never bring the snow ❀ I might make a little thunder ❀ But not very loud ❀ I think it would be grand to be a cloud

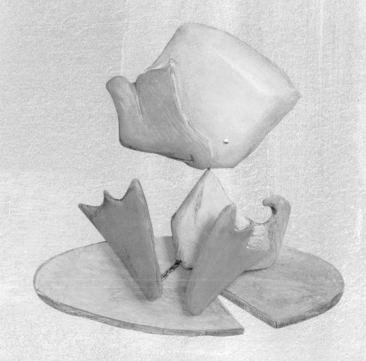

Story, lyrics, music and lead vocal Connie Kaldor ☀ Record Producer Paul Campagne ☀
Artistic Director Roland Stringer ☀ Illustrations Fil et Julie ☀ Graphic Design Haus Design
Communications ☀ Score Transcription Marc Ouellette ☀ Translation Roland Stringer ☀
Story Consultants Mona Cochingyan, Edith Skewes-Cox and Karen Alliston Musicians Connie
Kaldor piano, jug, keyboard bass, Rhodes ☀ Paul Campagne acoustic and electric guitar, bass,
ukulele, sound effects, whistle, percussion, timpani ☀ Davy Gallant drums, bass, percussions,
mandolin, juice harp, bongos, dumbek, flute, banjo, harmonica ☀ Bob Cohen electric guitar
Luigi Alamano trombone, trumpet, euphonium, trombone ☀ Jonathan Moorman violin
Aleksi Campagne ukulele Vocals and vocal effects Paul Campagne *Belly Button, Seed In The
Ground, Slug Opera, Quack, Quack, Quack* ☀ Gabriel Campagne *If You Love a Hippopotamus,
Laundry Bag, Belly Button, Honey, Honey, Honey, I Love Tomatoes, Quack, Quack, Quack*
Aleksi Campagne *If You Love a Hippopotamus, Laundry Bag, Belly Button, Honey, Honey,
Honey, I Love Tomatoes, Quack, Quack, Quack* ☀ Émilie-Rachel Stringer *I Love Tomatoes,
Laundry Bag* ☀ Thomas Stringer *I Love Tomatoes, Laundry Bag* ☀ Recorded by Paul Campagne
and Davy Gallant at Studio King and Dogger Pond Studio ☀ Mixed by Davy Gallant at Dogger
Pond Studio ☀ Mastered by Renée Marc-Aurèle at SNB

www.thesecretmountain.com ☀ ISBN 2-923163-02-8 ☀ All rights reserved ☀ No part of this book may be reproduced or
transmitted in any form or by any means, electronic or mechanical, including photocopying, recording, or by any information storage
or retrieval system, without permission in writing from the copyright holder. ☀ Printed in Hong Kong, China by Book Art Inc., Toronto
☀ We acknowledge the financial support of the Government of Canada through the Canada Music Fund for this project.